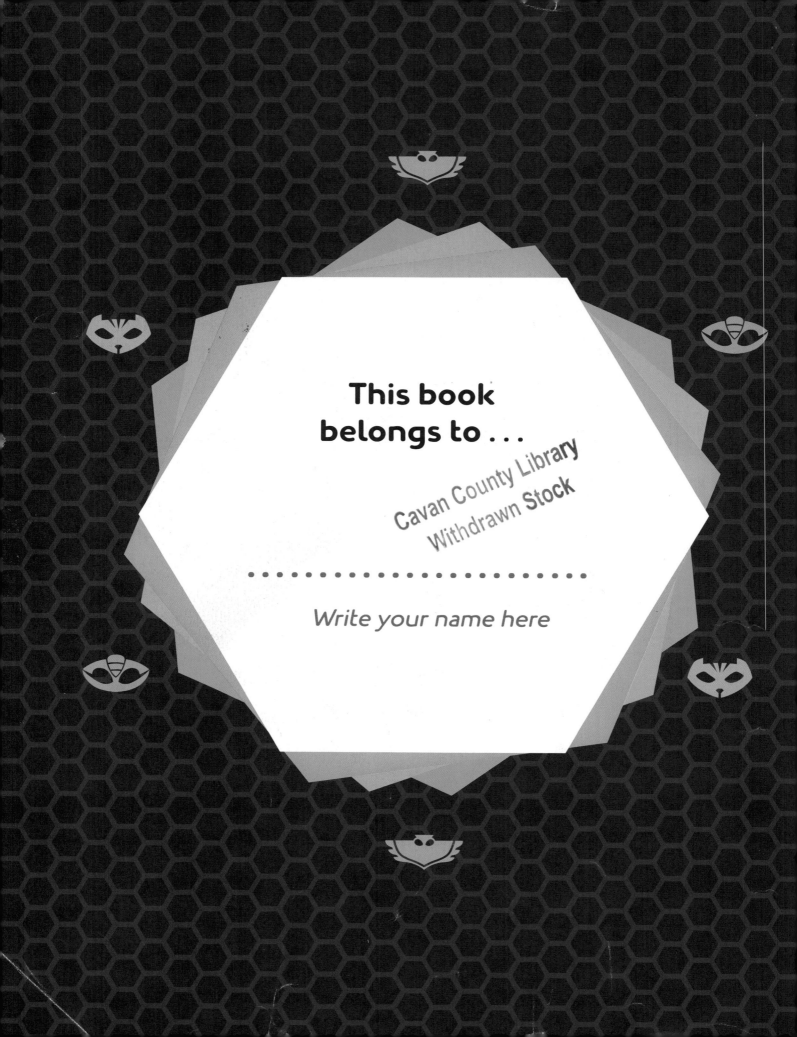

This book belongs to . . .

. . . .

Write your name here

PJMASKS

ANNUAL 2020

pat a Cake

CONTENTS

HERE COME THE PJ MASKS

Colour in the heroes so they are ready for adventure!

ARE YOU READY FOR AN ADVENTURE?
FLIP THE PAGE AS FAST AS YOU CAN!

GO! GO! GO!

It's time to be a hero! Look really carefully at the two pictures and use your super-sight Owl Eyes to work out the five differences between them.

GREG BECOMES GEKKO!

CONNOR BECOMES CATBOY!

AMAYA BECOMES OWLETTE!

MOONFIZZLED!

Uh-oh. Luna Girl has flung her pesky pink brainwashing balls everywhere! Can you spot who has been Moonfizzled tonight?

ANSWER

....

9

NINJA FINGER GAME

Night Ninja can get himself into all kinds of tight spots. Try this game and test out your flexible fingers!

USE THIS PICTURE TO WORK OUT WHICH FINGER TO USE. IF YOU ROLL A TWO, PUT YOUR POINTER FINGER ON THE BOARD.

How to Play

1 Sit either side of the board and choose which hand you are going to use to roll and which you will use to play.

2 The youngest player goes first. Each player must roll the dice twice. On the first roll, the number tells you which finger to use. The second roll tells you which row to move to.

3 Rolling a six means you get to roll again!

4 The winner is the first player to get all of their fingers on different rows of the board.

1 2 3 4 5

11

SEARCH HQ

All the PJ Masks characters are hiding inside HQ. Use your super powers to find them all – and their enemies!

Catboy ☐

Gekko ☐

Owlette ☐

PJ Robot ☐

Luna Girl ☐

Night Ninja ☐

Romeo ☐

O	E	M	O	R	H	P
O	H	Q	Q	N	Q	J
B	W	H	G	I	L	R
H	Q	L	P	G	B	O
J	F	U	E	H	H	B
H	Q	N	K	T	Q	O
E	Q	A	Q	N	T	T
X	H	G	H	I	G	E
D	P	I	B	N	E	Q
Q	H	R	Y	J	K	H
C	T	L	R	A	K	X
L	C	A	T	B	O	Y

TIP

THE NAMES COULD BE HIDDEN IN ANY DIRECTION SO LOOK CLOSELY! DID YOU FIND THEM ALL?

CATBOY'S CODE

Sometimes things get so tricky and sticky the PJ Masks have to use a secret code to make plans. Can you crack Catboy's code and save the day?

AT	**ROMEO**	**HURRY**	**SPLAT**	**NEED**	**OWLETTE**

FURBALLS	**HERO**	**HQ**	**PLEASE**	**TRAP**	**ATTACK**

_____	_____	_____	_____	_____	_____

GEKKO V NINJA

Would you take on the mighty Night Ninja? In this game you race to see who can get three in a row first. Do you dare?

How to Play

 Decide who is going to be Gekko and who is going to be Night Ninja.

 Sit either side of the board and keep your counters close.

 Take turns to place a counter on the board. Each player is trying to make a line of three, either up, down or across the board.

 The first player to make a line of three is the winner!

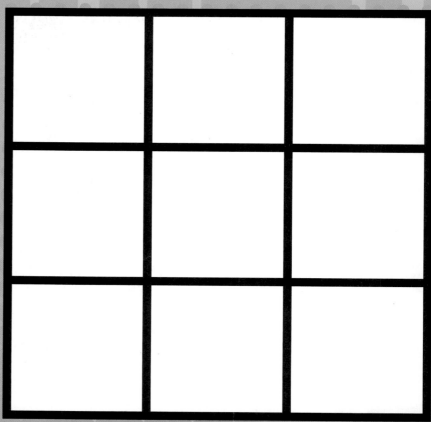

14

HOW ARE YOU FEELING?

Every day is different for the PJ Masks! Can you draw a face in the circles below to show how you think the PJ Masks are feeling?

THE FIRST ONE HAS BEEN DONE FOR YOU

OWLETTE'S MAGIC SQUARES

This game will really test your amazing Owl Eyes!
It's not as easy as it looks, so get ready!

HOW MANY PURPLE SQUARES CAN YOU COUNT HERE?

WHY NOT CHALLENGE A FRIEND?

EXTRA CHALLENGE: HOW MANY MOTHS CAN YOU SPOT?

LET'S GET MOVING!

Catboy knows it's important to stay nimble to outwit the night-time villains! He loves to keep the PJ Masks on their toes with this game.

THIS WILL EXERCISE YOUR BRAIN AND YOUR BODY!

What To Do:

1 Each player should choose which character they want to be.

2 The youngest player starts. He or she calls out Catboy's name followed by an instruction, for example: "Catboy says jump up high!"

3 Now everyone playing jumps up high.

4 The other players must obey ALL the commands that begin with "Catboy says".

5 If you call out an instruction without saying "Catboy says", all players have to STAY STILL!

6 If you get it wrong, you're out of the game.

7 The winner is the last PJ Masks hero standing!

SOME IDEAS FOR COMMANDS:

JUMP UP AND DOWN

STAND ON ONE LEG

TOUCH YOUR TOES

SHOUT "IT'S TIME TO BE A HERO!"

WAVE YOUR ARMS

KNEEL DOWN

YOU CAN PLAY THIS GAME WITH ONE OTHER PERSON OR A WHOLE GROUP!

19

ROBOT RESCUE

Romeo is trying to zap Gekko at the end of the maze. Help PJ Robot save him! Be careful though – if he takes the wrong path he'll end up with Romeo or his Robot!

SCAN AND SEEK

There are PJ heroes and dark villains hidden in this box.
Can you find them and draw a line through them? The first
one has been done for you. Beware of the Ninjalinos!

Five Luna Girls ☐   Four Owlettes ☐

Three Moon Balls ☐   Three Catboys ☐

Two Romeos ☐   Three Luna Magnets ☐

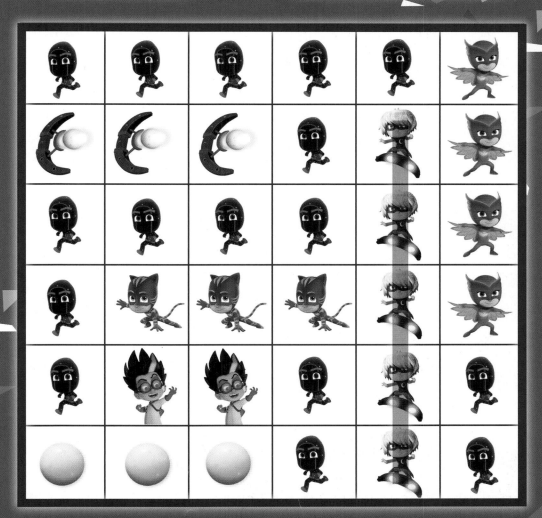

TIP

THEY COULD BE HIDDEN SIDE-TO-SIDE TOO!

OWL EYES!

Owlette has super-amazing eyesight, but how good is yours? Look at these close-ups and spot where they fit in the big picture.

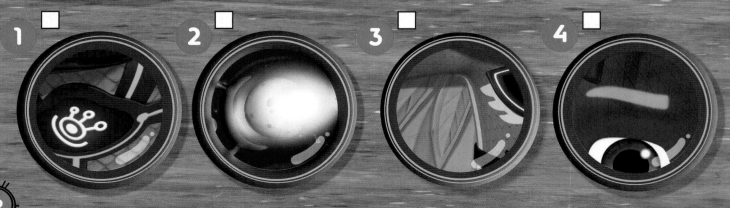

1 □

2 □

3 □

4 □

ROMEO'S PICTURE PUZZLE

Each row and column as well as each of the four large squares should contain one PJ hero. Work out who should be in each of the empty squares.

BALANCE LIKE A NINJA!

Night Ninja is the balance king. Try these tricky tricks to test your skills.

BALANCE SKILLS

⭐ Lay out some paper on the floor to make a long straight line.

⭐ First just try walking along it. Stay on the paper – no toes over the edge!

⭐ Easy? Okay – now try walking backwards along it.

⭐ No problem? Try hopping all the way along.

⭐ Night Ninja's challenge: Walk all the way along with your eyes closed!

TIP
Are you a balance master?
Try with a piece of paper half the width!

ASK A GROWN UP BEFORE YOU PLAY.

ONE FOOT WONDER

⭐ Even Night Ninja finds this one difficult. He practises with Ninjalinos and sometimes he drops them!

⭐ Collect different bits and pieces from around your home – you could try a cushion, a marble, and more. Nothing breakable! Then find a container, like a basket or a bucket.

⭐ Carefully balance an object on one of your feet. Lift up your foot and drop the object into the bucket.

TIP
⭐ Take your shoes off!
⭐ You can play this alone or challenge a friend.

REMEMBER TO PUT EVERYTHING BACK!

IT'S TIME TO BE A HERO!

PJMASKS

ARE YOU A PJ MASKS MASTER?

HOW WELL DO YOU KNOW THE PJ MASKS?

2
Luna Girl builds a fortress under the sea.
True ⬤ False ⬤

1
The PJ Masks' HQ can turn into a rocket.
True ⬤ False ⬤

4
The PJ Masks each have a special PJ Rover for getting about on the Moon.
True ⬤ False ⬤

3
Luna Girl has little moth helpers.
True ⬤ False ⬤

5
PJ Robot helps the PJ Masks from the HQ.
True ⬤ False ⬤

SPEEDY WHEELS

Who is this whizzing into the night to save the day?
Grab a pencil and join the dots to find out.
Now colour in the picture and add some
stars and a moon.

WHICH WAY OUT?

The Wolfy Kids are on the prowl. Help Catboy find the right path to chase each one down and OUT OF TOWN!

CATBOY NEEDS TO PICK UP EACH WOLFY KID AS HE RUNS THROUGH THE MAZE.

START

OUT OF TOWN

SPEED SURGE!

29

PAW COOKIES

CATBOY IS AS QUICK AS A CAT! MIX UP A BATCH OF THESE CUTE PAW COOKIES FOR YOUR FRIENDS. THEY'LL SMELL A LOT BETTER THAN CATBOY'S FEET!

INGREDIENTS

220g self raising flour
120g softened butter
100g caster sugar
1 egg
½ teaspoon vanilla essence
Giant chocolate buttons

3
Add the egg and the vanilla essence.

6
Ask an adult to take them out of the oven and cool for a few minutes.

1
Ask an adult to pre-heat the oven to 180 degrees celsius.

2
In a big bowl, beat together the butter and the sugar.

4
Roll the mixture into balls and place on a baking tray lined with non-stick paper. Squash each one down a little bit.

5
Bake for 8-10 minutes or until light brown in colour.

7
Stick a chocolate button at the bottom of each biscuit.

8
Break some more buttons in half and push into the cookie for claws.

TIP

It's important that the cookies are still soft when you decorate them because it will help the buttons stick. If the cookies are too cool, you could use a blob of chocolate spread or melted chocolate to help the buttons stick!

31

WHAT'S YOUR ID?

Create your own identity card so everyone can gasp at your awesome superhero status!

YOUR PORTRAIT

SUPERHERO NAME:

....

....

SUPER ABILITIES

POWER RATING

Strength: ☆ ☆ ☆ ☆ ☆

Speed: ☆ ☆ ☆ ☆ ☆

Agility: ☆ ☆ ☆ ☆ ☆

Stamina: ☆ ☆ ☆ ☆ ☆

Brain power: ☆ ☆ ☆ ☆ ☆

COLOUR IN THE STARS TO SHOW YOUR POWER RATING

READY, STEADY, COLOUR!

Where are the PJ Masks?
Find the dots below and colour them in to reveal the heroes!
Now add their names to the picture.

USE THE SAME
COLOUR AS
THE DOT!

....

33

SUPERHERO CHALLENGE

CRAWL ACROSS THE ROOM AND BACK

BALANCE ON ONE FOOT FOR TEN SECONDS

ROLL IN A STRAIGHT LINE ACROSS THE ROOM AND BACK

JUMP AS HIGH AS YOU CAN TEN TIMES

SIT AND THEN STAND UP TEN TIMES

RUN ON THE SPOT FOR TEN SECONDS

WALK BACKWARDS FOR TEN STEPS

It's tough being a superhero and Owlette, Gekko and Catboy need to be quick and strong to save the day! Check out their routine and choose five actions to do every day!

BEND DOWN AND TOUCH YOUR TOES TEN TIMES

MIX IT UP EVERY DAY AND CHALLENGE A FRIEND!

JUMP AS FAR AS YOU CAN FIVE TIMES KEEPING BOTH FEET TOGETHER

HOP ON ONE FOOT TEN TIMES

PJ ROVERS

The PJ Masks have super-cool PJ Rovers for exploring the Moon. Use your pencils or crayons to colour them in.

LET'S GO!

Sometimes you just have to escape FAST! The Owl Glider, Cat-Car and the Gekko Mobile will always come to the rescue!

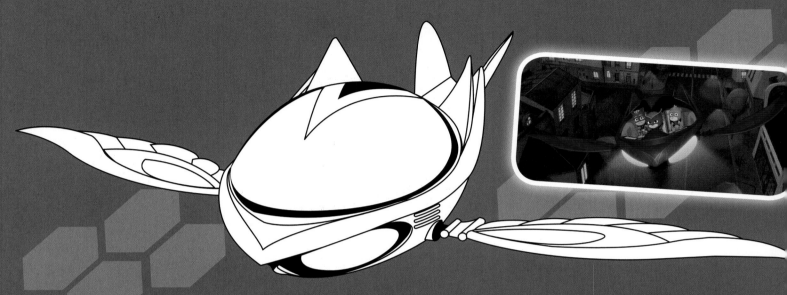

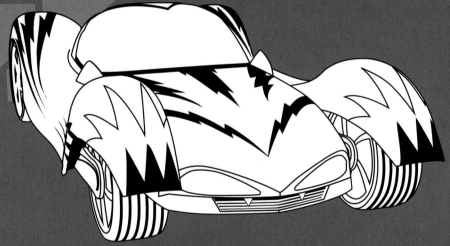

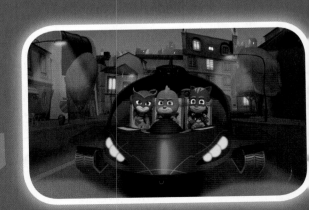

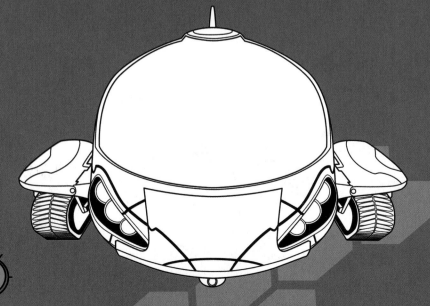

ROVERS TO THE RESCUE

The PJ Masks also have special PJ Rovers to help them get around on the Moon. What would your PJ Rover look like? Draw it in here, then colour it in – don't forget to add yourself as a PJ hero!

CHARACTER COUNT!

Here are LOTS of PJ Masks heroes and villains.
Colour them in and count them up.

Write your answers in the boxes below!

GUESS WHO?

Can you work out who's who? Look at the shadows and consider the clues, it's time to be a hero!

1 This hero can catch villains with his Super Cat Stripes.

2 This super-stealthy villain has lots of little squeaky followers.

3 This PJ Mask has Super Camouflage power.

4 This brainbox baddie loves inventing new things.

5

This soaring superstar can see things from far away.

....

6

This PJ friend helps the heroes out of sticky spots.

....

7

This fiendish flier wants to take over the world ... from the Moon.

....

8

This trio of baddies have a super-strong sense of smell.

....

9

This tough guy tries to help the PJ Masks.

....

FRIENDS FOREVER!

Join the dots and watch as two PJ heroes are revealed.

COLOUR THEM IN, TOO!

TRAP TRICK!

Poor Owlette! Night Ninja has caught her with his sticky splats. Help her find the way out to safety, and avoid all the Ninjalino pests on the way!

START

FINISH

LUNA GIRL'S MAGNET MAYHEM!

Watch out! Luna Girl has turned her menacing magnet onto you! Don't let her pull you up to her Luna Board. You MUST resist!

PLAYER ONE

| 1 | 2 Move forward two spaces. | 3 | 4 | 5 Miss a turn. | 6 Move back 5 spaces. | 7 | 8 Zap! You've been pulled up the lunar beam! | 9 |

PLAYER TWO

| 1 | 2 | 3 Move foward one space. | 4 | 5 Miss a turn. | 6 | 7 Move back three spaces. | 8 Zap! You've been pulled up the lunar beam! | 9 |

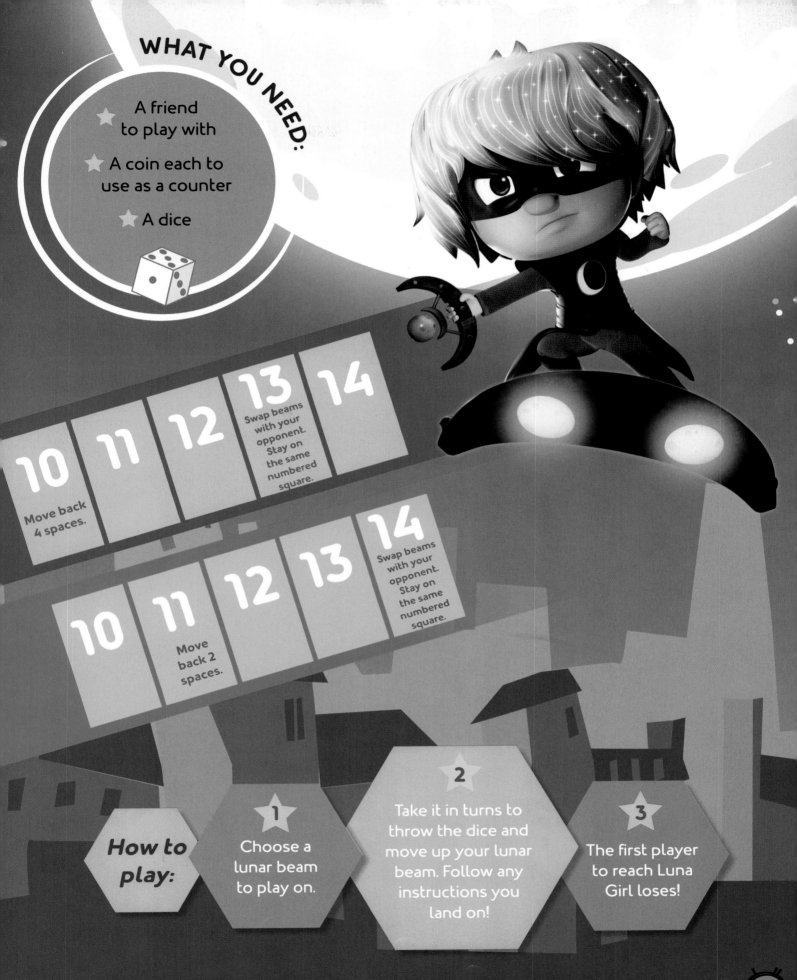

★ A friend to play with

★ A coin each to use as a counter

★ A dice

10

11

12

13 Swap beams with your opponent. Stay on the same numbered square.

14

Move back 4 spaces.

10

11 Move back 2 spaces.

12

13

14 Swap beams with your opponent. Stay on the same numbered square.

How to play:

⭐ 1 Choose a lunar beam to play on.

2 Take it in turns to throw the dice and move up your lunar beam. Follow any instructions you land on!

⭐ 3 The first player to reach Luna Girl loses!

47

WHICH WOLFY?

You would recognise Howler in a crowd, but what about a crowd of Howlers? Look closely at these pictures and draw a line connecting the two identical pictures.

CATCHPHRASE QUIZ

Each PJ Mask hero and villain has a catchphrase or two!
Choose one of the words below to fill in the gaps and then
draw a line connecting each phrase to a character.

1. SUPER _____ SPEED!
2. LEAPING _____ !
3. ___ WING WIND!
4. I'M THE CAT'S _____ !
5. _____ GEKKO MUSCLES!
6. _____ FEATHERS!

WHISKERS

CAT

LIZARDS

OWL

FLUTTERING

SUPER

ROMEO BRAIN TANGLER

Romeo can tie your brain in knots with his clever plots and schemes. Amaze your friends with his amazing magic number trick!

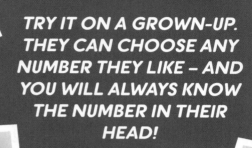

TRY IT ON A GROWN-UP. THEY CAN CHOOSE ANY NUMBER THEY LIKE – AND YOU WILL ALWAYS KNOW THE NUMBER IN THEIR HEAD!

1 ASK YOUR FRIEND TO THINK OF A NUMBER AND KEEP IT IN THEIR HEAD.

2 NOW ASK THEM TO DOUBLE IT.

ANSWER ....

3 ADD TEN.

ANSWER ....

4 HALVE THIS NUMBER.

ANSWER ....

5 NOW THEY SHOULD TAKE AWAY THE NUMBER THEY STARTED WITH.

NOW YOU CAN PRETEND TO BE THINKING REALLY HARD, LIKE ROMEO WOULD, AND TELL THEM THAT THE NUMBER THEY HAVE NOW IS 5!

TIP

START WITH CHOOSING A NUMBER UNDER TEN.

I'LL GET YOU, PJ MASKS!

Inside his lab, Romeo has seen the PJ Masks getting away. He chases them but crashes his lab and breaks his screen! Work out which piece completes the picture.

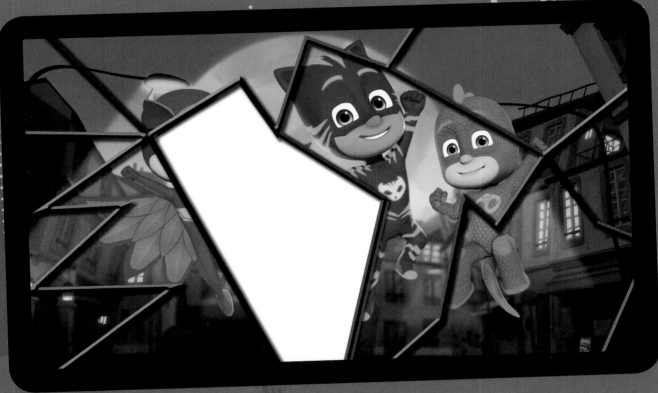

1

2

3

ROBOT LOVE

Romeo really loves to hug! Look carefully at all these pictures and work out which two are the same.

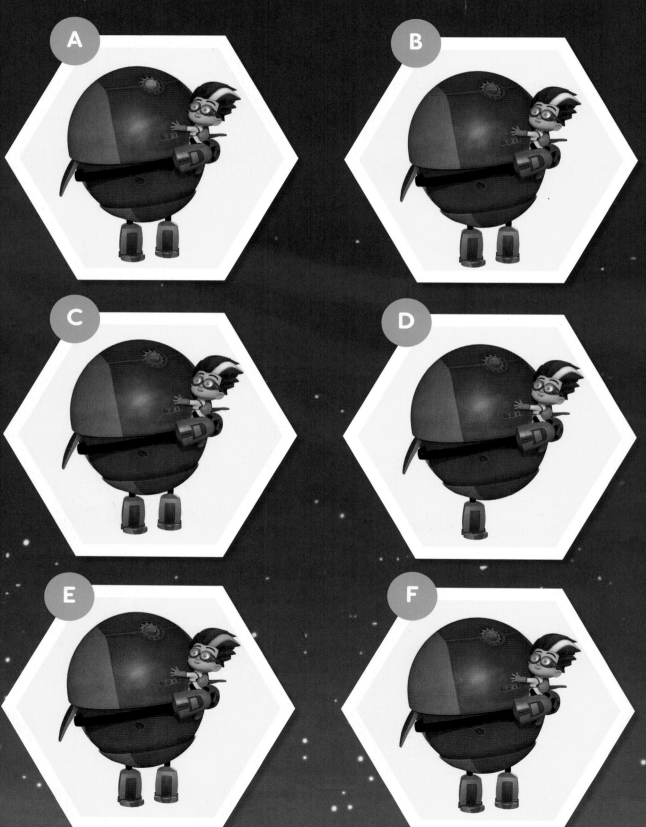

OWLETTE'S CROSS QUIZ

Owlette has set you a challenge! Can you fit each of these PJ Masks names into the grid?

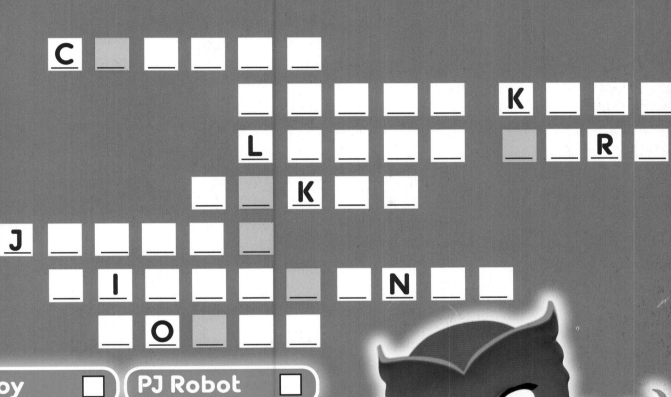

Catboy	☐	PJ Robot	☐
Wolfy Kids	☐	Night Ninja	☐
Lunar Girl	☐	Romeo	☐
Gekko	☐		

NOW REARRANGE THE BLUE SQUARES TO MAKE A WORD!

ANSWER ....

FUN AT THE PARK

★ Look at the picture and help your favourite heroes answer the questions.

Which PJ Masks vehicles are missing?

Are there any moths in the picture?

Can you count the stars?

ARE YOU JOKING?

Here are some great jokes to share with your PJ fan friends!

Why wasn't the butterfly allowed into the party? *Because it was a moth ball!*

What do you call an owl with a really deep voice? *A growl!*

What kind of tiles can't you stick on walls? *Reptiles!*

What is harder to catch the faster you run? *Your breath!*

What are Night Ninja's favourite cookies? *Ninjabread Men!*

WORD WORKOUT

Lunar Girl has scrambled up all of the words below!
Can you help the heroes unscramble the words?

1 ⭐ GNAMTE

2 ⭐ BOTRO

3 ⭐ ETOLWTE

4 ⭐ KKOEG

5 ⭐ BACTOY

SPACE RACE

The PJ Masks are in space! Help them zoom to the moon through the maze.

START

FINISH

PJ SEEKER

The PJ Masks have a super-cool new super-vehicle. Can you colour in the PJ Seeker? Use the little picture to help you. Ready, steady, go!

ANSWERS

Page 8
GO! GO! GO!

Page 9
Moonfizzled

ANSWER

GEKKO

Page 12
Search HQ

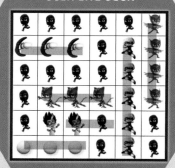

Page 13
Catboy's Code

SPLAT   ATTACK   AT

HQ   PLEASE   HURRY

Page 17
Owlette's Magic Squares

ANSWER

5

EXTRA GAME:
5 moths are hidden

Page 21
Scan and Seek

Page 22
Owl Eyes

Page 20
Robot Rescue

Page 23
Romeo's Picture Puzzle

Page 27
Are You a PJ Masks Master?

1 = TRUE
2 = FALSE
3 = TRUE
4 = TRUE
5 = TRUE

Page 29
Which Way Out

Page 41
Character Count

2   2   2   2   3

Pages 42-43
Guess Who?

1. CATBOY
2. NIGHT NINJA
3. GEKKO
4. ROMEO
5. OWLETTE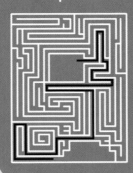
6. PJ ROBOT
7. LUNA GIRL
8. WOLFY KIDS
9. ARMADYLAN

Page 45
Trap Trick

Page 48
Which Wolfy?

ANSWER
B&F

Page 49
Catchphrase Quiz

1 = CATBOY
2 = GEKKO
3 = OWLETTE
4 = CATBOY
5 = GEKKO
6 = OWLETTE

Page 51
I'll get you, PJ Masks!

3

Page 52
Robot Love!

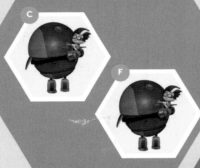

C

F

Page 53
Owlette's Cross Quiz

```
C A T B O Y
    W O L F Y   K I D S
    L U N A R   G I R L
    G E K K O
P J R O B O T
N I G H T N I N J A
R O M E O
```

NEW WORD:
MAGNET

Page 57
Word Workout

1 = MAGNET
2 = ROBOT
3 = OWLETTE
4 = GEKKO
5 = CATBOY

Page 58
Space Race

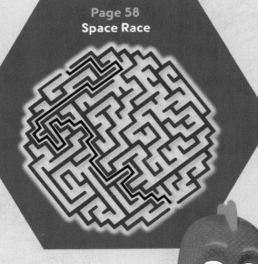

PJ MASKS, ALL
SHOUT HOORAY!
'COS IN THE NIGHT,
WE SAVED THE DAY!